A Monster on the Street

Part 2

written by Jeremy Strong
illustrated by Steve Smallman

Chapter One

Ben has an idea

"What can we do?" yelled Mouse. "There'll be a crash!" The piano was lumbering towards them. The man on top was shouting. "Quick," shouted Ben. "Give me your jumpers."

The friends pulled off their jumpers.
"What are you going to do?" asked Jojo.

Ben just grabbed the jumpers and threw
them into the middle of the road.

"What did you do that for?" demanded
Donut, staring at his best jumper.
"It might not work," said Ben. "But it's
the only thing I can think of."

They watched with popping eyes as the piano thundered down the road. The other removal men chased after it.

A man was so shocked he fell off his bike.

One of the piano wheels hit the pile of jumpers. The wheel jammed as one jumper was dragged round and round and the piano lumbered across the road.

"Woa!" yelled the man on top. He slid across the lid and was thrown clear. The piano skidded to one side and came to a stop.

The removal men came running up,
panting hard.
"That was a very clever thing to do,"
said one of them. He patted Ben's back.
Ben shrugged.

"We were lucky it worked," he said shyly.
"Very lucky," agreed the men.
"Don't ever ask me to move a piano again,"
said the one who had ridden on the top.

By this time a small crowd had come to see what all the fuss was about. Donut and Cleo's parents came running down the road. Cassandra Pringle looked rather like Cleo, only bigger. She had long dark hair too, and lots of bangles.

Mrs Pringle swept Cleo into her arms.
"Oh my little darling! Are you all right?"
She kissed Cleo again and again.

Mrs Pringle's giant earrings kept banging in
Cleo's face. Cleo struggled to escape.

"She's fine," said Colin, their step-father,
with a chuckle. "Come on, princess."

Cleo stamped her foot. "I'm not a princess.
I'm a queen," she hissed.
"I do beg your pardon, Your Highness,"
said Mr Pringle. The others laughed.

"It's not funny!" cried Cleo,
stamping her foot again.
"I'm just glad you're all
okay," said Mr Pringle.

Mrs Pringle suddenly put both hands to her face. "I know!" she said, turning to the children. "You are all so kind. You children must come to tea!"

The children stared in horror at Donut.
They knew Mrs Pringle was a terrible cook.

Chapter Two
Tea with the Queen

Donut began to panic.
"No Mum, no."
Mrs Pringle was puzzled.
"What do you mean?"
"Um, you're much too busy.
We're still moving in."
"Nonsense," said Mrs Pringle.
"Your friends must come to
tea." Mrs Pringle beamed
happily at them. The children
followed Mrs Pringle silently
into the new house.
"We're all going to die,"
whispered the Queen
of Sheba.

The house was at
sixes and sevens.

Packing cases were
piled in every room.

THIS
WAY
UP

LOFT

Mrs Pringle showed the
children into the kitchen.
She began pulling food
out of boxes.
"I know, I will make you
peanut butter omelettes."

PEANUT BUTTER

FRESH EGGS

Kitchen

Donut groaned, but Sam sat down at the table. "That will be very nice," she said politely. Mrs Pringle ruffled Sam's hair. "Good girl," she said, and turned to the others. "Come on, sit down. Cleo, why are you lying on the floor?"

"I'm dead," Cleo said. "Dead people don't eat omelettes."

"Don't be silly, get up at once."

The peanut butter omelettes arrived.

"Yum," said Donut. As soon as his mother wasn't looking he tipped his plate out of the window.

"Yum, yum," said Cleo. As soon as her mother wasn't looking she tipped her omelette onto Donut's empty plate.

"Come on Donut, eat up,"
said Mrs Pringle.
The friends giggled.

Donut waited until
Mrs Pringle turned
her back.
He slipped the
second omelette
inside a flower vase.

19

The others ate their omelettes -
s l o w l y - they were very chewy.

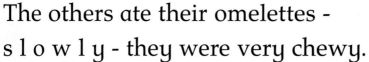

Ben finished his first.
"Would you like some more?"
asked Mrs Pringle.
"Um, no thank you. I'm so full.
I couldn't eat another thing."

The children finished their food.
"Thank you," said Mouse.
"That was lovely."
"You must come again,"
smiled Mrs Pringle.
"You are such polite children.
It is so nice to find people who
enjoy my cooking. I will make
you something special.
How about chicken stuffed
with marshmallows?"

When they were back on Story Street
Jojo turned to Donut.
"Does your mum always cook things
like that?"

Donut shook his head. "No," he said.
"That was one of her best meals.

You should have seen what we had to eat
last week ..."

Mrs Pringle's recipes